For Noreen
M.W.

First published 1989 by
Walker Books Ltd, 87 Vauxhall Walk
London SE11 5HJ

This edition published 1990

6 8 10 9 7

Text © 1989 Martin Waddell
Illustrations © 1989 Barbara Firth

Printed in Hong Kong

British Library Cataloguing in Publication Data
A catalogue record for this book is
available from the British Library.

ISBN 0-7445-1740-0

THIS WALKER BOOK BELONGS TO:

_____

_____

_____

_____

The Park in the Dark

written by
Martin Waddell

illustrated by
Barbara Firth

WALKER BOOKS
AND SUBSIDIARIES
LONDON • BOSTON • SYDNEY

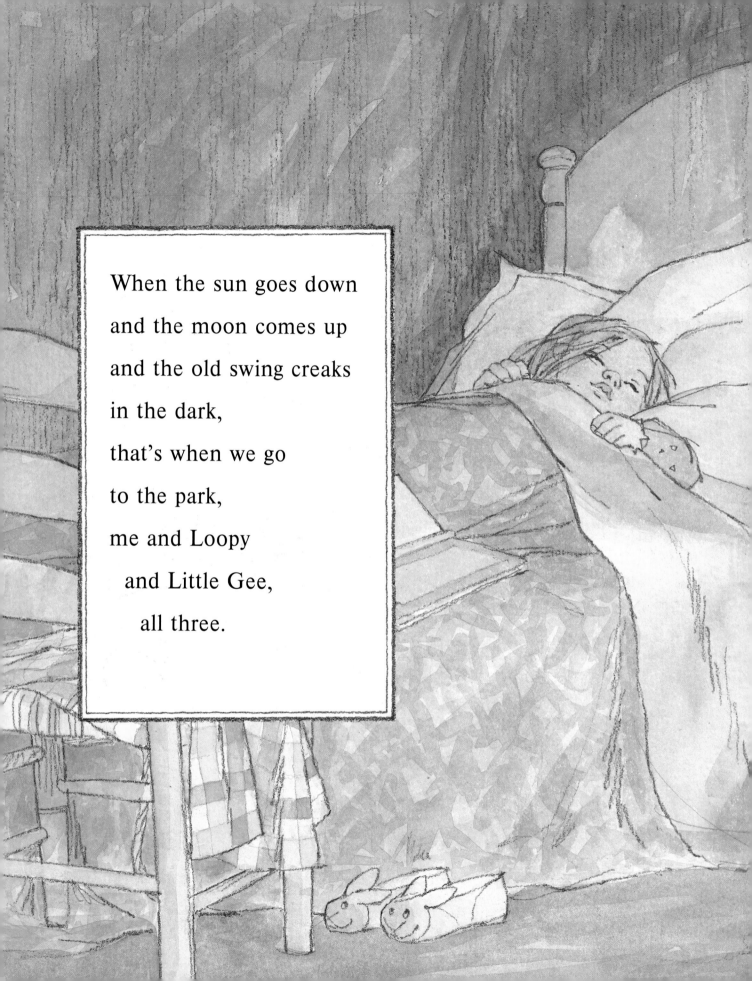

When the sun goes down
and the moon comes up
and the old swing creaks
in the dark,
that's when we go
to the park,
me and Loopy
and Little Gee,
all three.

Softly down the staircase,

through the haunty hall,

trying to look

small,

me and Loopy

and Little Gee,

we three.

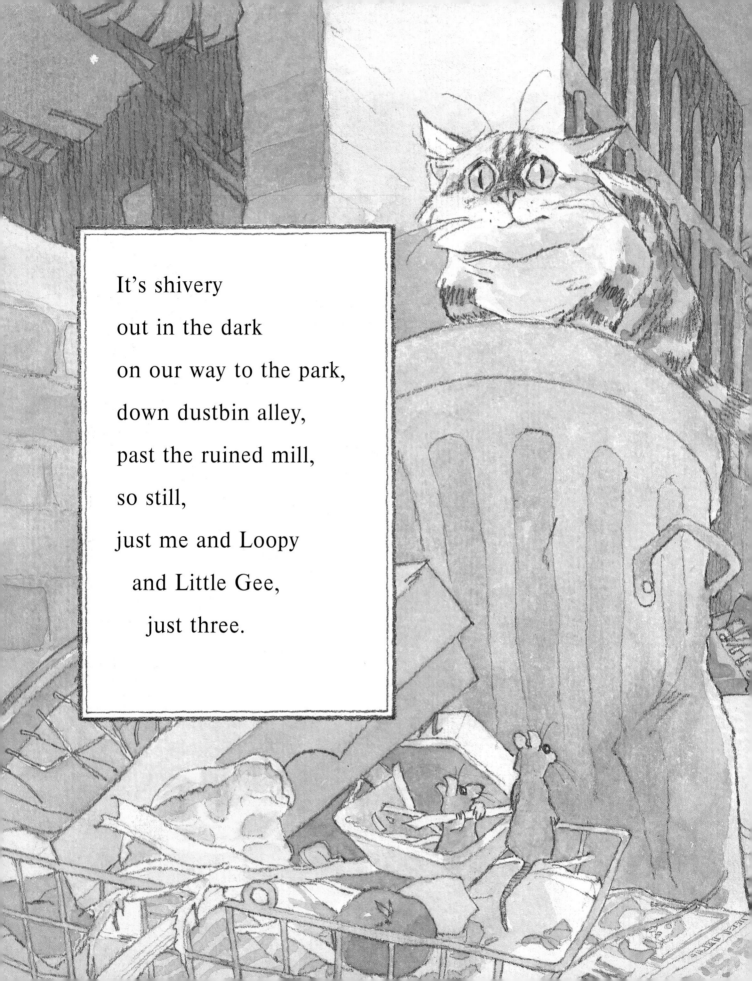

It's shivery

out in the dark

on our way to the park,

down dustbin alley,

past the ruined mill,

so still,

just me and Loopy

  and Little Gee,

    just three.

And Little Gee
doesn't like it.
He's scared
of the things
he might see
in the park
in the dark
with Loopy and me.
That's me and Loopy
and Little Gee,
the three.

There might be

moon witches

or man-eating trees

or withers that wobble

or old Scrawny Shins

or hairy hobgoblins,

or black boggarts' knees

in the trees,

or things we can't see,

me and Loopy

and Little Gee,

all three.

But there's not,
says Loopy,
and I agree,
and Little Gee
gets up on my back and
we pass the Howl Tree,
me and Loopy
and Little Gee.
We're heroes,
we three.

In the park

in the dark

by the lake

and the bridge,

that's when we see

where we want to be,

me and Loopy

and Little Gee.

WHOOPEE!

And we swing
and we slide
and we dance
and we jump
and we chase
all over the place,
me and Loopy
and Little Gee,
the Big Three!

And then
the THING comes!
YAAAAA
AAAIII
OOOOOEEEEEEE!

RUN RUN RUN
shouts Little Gee
to Loopy and me
and we
flee,
me and Loopy
   and Little Gee,
     scared three.

Back where we've come
through the park
in the dark
and the THING
is roaring
and following,
see?
After me and Loopy
    and Little Gee,
        we three.

Up to the house,
to the stair,
to the bed
where we ought to be,
me and Loopy
and Little Gee,
safe as can be,
all three.

MORE WALKER PAPERBACKS
For You to Enjoy
Also by Martin Waddell

CAN'T YOU SLEEP, LITTLE BEAR?
illustrated by Barbara Firth

Winner of the Smarties Book Prize and Kate Greenaway Medal

"The most perfect children's book ever written or illustrated." *The Sunday Times*

0-7445-1316-2   £4.99

THE TOUGH PRINCESS
illustrated by Patrick Benson

Shortlisted for the Children's Book Award

"Breaks all the conventions of the traditional fairy tale…
Spirited and energetic colour pictures add further humour
to this highly enjoyable story." *Child Education*

0-7445-1226-3   £4.99

OWL BABIES
illustrated by Patrick Benson

On a tree in the woods, three baby owls, Sarah and Percy and Bill, wait for their
Owl Mother to come home.

"Touchingly beautiful… The perfect picture book." *The Guardian*

0-7445-3167-5   £4.99

THE PIG IN THE POND
illustrated by Jill Barton

Highly commended for the Kate Greenaway Medal

One hot day, an amazing event occurs on Nelligan's farm.

"Pure fun… An excellent combination of text and illustration
with a satisfying finale." *The Daily Telegraph*

0-7445-3167-5   £4.99

Walker Paperbacks are available from most booksellers, or by post from B.B.C.S., P.O. Box 941, Hull, North Humberside HU1 3YQ

24 hour telephone credit card line 01482 224626

To order, send: Title, author, ISBN number and price for each book ordered, your full name and address,
cheque or postal order payable to BBCS for the total amount and allow the following for postage and packing:
UK and BFPO: £1.00 for the first book, and 50p for each additional book to a maximum of £3.50.
Overseas and Eire: £2.00 for the first book, £1.00 for the second and 50p for each additional book.

Prices and availability are subject to change without notice.